Robert Treat Paine

Pauperism in Great Cities

Its four chief causes

Robert Treat Paine

Pauperism in Great Cities
Its four chief causes

ISBN/EAN: 9783337426750

Printed in Europe, USA, Canada, Australia, Japan

Cover: Foto ©Andreas Hilbeck / pixelio.de

More available books at **www.hansebooks.com**

PAUPERISM IN GREAT CITIES.

ITS FOUR CHIEF CAUSES.

BY

ROBERT TREAT PAINE,

PRESIDENT OF THE ASSOCIATED CHARITIES OF BOSTON, THE AMERICAN
PEACE SOCIETY, THE WELLS MEMORIAL WORKINGMEN'S INSTITUTE,
THE WORKINGMEN'S COÖPERATIVE BANK, THE WORKINGMEN'S
BUILDING ASSOCIATION, THE WORKINGMEN'S LOAN ASSOCIATION,
THE BETTER DWELLINGS SOCIETY, FOUNDER AND PRESI-
DENT OF THE PEOPLES INSTITUTE, VICE PRESIDENT
OF THE BOSTON CHILDREN'S AID SOCIETY, ETC.

AUTHOR OF

Charity Organization,	Not Alms but a Friend,
Coöperative Banks,	Homes for the People,

How to Repress Pauperism, Etc.

READ AT THE INTERNATIONAL CONGRESS OF CHARITIES,
CORRECTION AND PHILANTHROPY, AT CHICAGO,

JUNE 12, 1893.

CONTENTS.

The problem of poor relief in great cities has got to be re-stated in ampler terms. The diseases of society are more aggravated, the dangers are graver, the need of radical remedies is more absolute, than the new Charity has yet fully and fairly faced.

This last quarter of a century has witnessed a noble outburst of the energies of good men to help suffering brethren.

"Science and sympathy" have been moved to do their utmost, under such fiery inspiration as that of Phillips Brooks when he threw the whole power of his support into the movement to create the Associated Charities of Boston. [Speech of March 12, 1879.]

The world is brighter and better for the devotion of the great galaxy of noble men and women all through the civilized world, who, seeing how the problem needs wisdom, bring to it deep and faithful study, and how it needs their sympathy and aid, bring to it loving devotion.

These are the men and women who are making this world fit to live in and this life worth living.

When the poor sink below their poverty into pauperism, and pauperism becomes hopeless and degraded and brutal; when powerful and prolific causes are at work to swell the rising tide; — the day has gone when it is enough to go on dealing with details.

Society must study till it knows the whole measure of the problem, seek whatever heroic measures can remedy the evils, and especially can cut off the supply, and invoke all the powers in our modern life of wisdom, energy and love, under the guidance and inspiration and with firm faith in the aid of God.

THE CONDITIONS OF LIFE

in our great cities excite deep concern. Pass them in brief review. The growth of city population, rapid and irresistible, compels the prophetic imagination to ask, but in vain, what is to be the limit of the number of souls in London and Paris, New York, Chicago and Philadelphia, and even in Baltimore and Boston.

With population, rents rise so that the average man, that is the masses of the people, are forced to live in utterly unfit homes, fearfully overcrowded; hence low vitality of body and soul, diseased morals and diseased bodies.

The extremes of society grow more pronounced, so that from the increasing numbers of the very poor, a larger residuum, Charles Booth's Submerged Tenth, Charles Loring Brace's Dangerous Classes, reach such proportions that they can no longer be dealt with in detail and hopefully as individuals, but fill up whole areas like that great ward in Liverpool, crowded with the dock laborers, where the level of life is at such uniform dead low tide, that to uplift a part is impossible without uplifting the general level of all, and the idea of uplifting the whole suggests attacking the Atlantic; to me the saddest spectacle of hopeless despair I have ever anywhere beheld, Liverpool's dead sea.

Society by its loving energies can deal with evils in detail, but who can find the remedy when evils of all kinds are aggregated into a vast mass at a uniform low level of degradation, destitution and despair.

Strong drink is almost the sole solace of their dull routine. Saturday night and Sunday find so many, that it seems a large proportion, sodden with drink, the aged as well as those in youth, even babies at the breast. Nay, let me recall the words of the Chief of Police as he took me through these sights of sadness, children begotten by drunken parents, born of drunken mothers, nursed by drinking mothers, and thus saturated with liquor from the start.

Crimes of violence, crimes of lust, crimes against property, not only prevail, but cease to shock, where the general level of life has lapsed into a new phase of barbarism.

What hope for boys and girls growing up in such atmosphere of sin, in overcrowded cities from which play grounds have been excluded by rising rents; play grounds for the innocent outpouring of the boys' animal spirits which will have some vent, if not in hockey and foot ball, then in breaking into empty buildings, stealing lead pipes and stoning dispensary doctors or police with even-handed delight.

Yet critics say "The Bitter Cry of Outcast London" is a bit overdrawn.

" We have opened but a little way the door that leads into this plague-house of sin and misery and corruption, where men and women and little children starve and suffer and perish, body and soul. We shall not wonder if some, shuddering at the revolting spectacle, try to persuade themselves that such things cannot be in Christian England, and that what they have looked upon is some dark vision conjured up by a morbid pity and a desponding faith. To such we can only say, Will you venture to come with us and see for yourselves the ghastly reality?" [Page 20.]

What is my conclusion? Shall I not say that in the largest cities where conditions are worst, and the evils of pauperism, grown chronic and contagious, are blended with habits of drunkenness and other vice, breaking out into crimes against the law, pauperism cannot be wisely considered alone, but the problem of how to uplift the general level of life must be studied *as one whole problem*, especially as to the causes of the evils.

Boston can speak words of encouragement. Boston is of just the size for the best study of the data, as well as a successful combination of forces for thorough, encouraging and permanent success. I rejoice to be able to say that in Boston, the conditions of life among working people, counting all, even those on the lowest levels, are on the whole visibly improving.

Does not this same encouraging condition prevail amongst most of the smaller cities of the United States? Have not the various agencies, working together for good in the social awakening and religious life of our times, attained such vigor that they are waging winning war against the forces which drag life down? On the whole, are not things mending rather than growing worse?

What more can I hope to achieve on this point than to fasten the acute observations of leaders in each city on this exact question, whether the *standard of life of working people* is rising or falling?

In New York and London, no doubt in Paris and Berlin, the data are largely different. I hope I am wrong when I express the fear that in these cities the general tide is still falling, in marked contrast to its rise in almost all other cities of less size.

But what hope is there for these four greatest cities, may I add Chicago, unless they are stirred to superhuman efforts, in part at least by candid and friendly criticism?

One main purpose of my paper is now to draw attention to this tremendous fact that

PAUPERISM IS ASSUMING A NEW AND MORE TERRIBLE TYPE

in the largest cities, where paupers have lived so long in this condition that they know nothing better; —

Where pauperism is hereditary and paupers are born into a condition not unlike the castes of India; whence there is no hope; and they are content with their lot, which varies with the seasons, tramping on lovely country roads in summer, robbing hen roosts or houses, perhaps from hunger or partly from delight in pleasurable excitement, increased by the risk of an encounter or of a month or two in a spacious building with all reasonable comfort, so much better than they get outside; —

Where out-relief, or private charity, or loose alms guarantee against serious suffering; —

And where, as in London and New York, their numbers are so large that, first, the evil influences they receive from each other far exceed any good influences which Christian society has yet learned to apply; second, their treatment in casual wards, almshouses, jails, reformatories or prisons, by police or officials, is — I had almost said of necessity,— almost always mechanical, and too often hard and brutalizing, as for instance in the casual wards*

---

*The Wayfarers' Lodge in Boston seems to unite such decent treatment of inmates with clean bed in ample rooms, fairly good food, with enforced bath and a stent of about three hours' labor in sawing wood in the morning, as to meet the present conditions of Pauperism in a city like Boston. The system is not so harsh that human citizens refuse to send casuals to the Lodge, nor so attractive as to promote vagrancy.

Wayfarers' Lodges have been established in Philadelphia and are proposed in New York, similar to that in Boston.

The earlier system, which prevailed of sending to Police Stations casuals who asked bed or food, has been generally condemned.

Shall we not agree that every city should have a lodge for wayfarers, combining humane treatment, enough though very simple food, clean bed, with insistence on a just return in labor from every able bodied man, and a full measure of genuine sympathy for those seeking work, nay for all, and especially with best possible counsel where to seek employment? Boston has its great Labor Bureau in an adjoining building.

of London with cold stone walls, in prison-like cells,— a stent of stone to be broken and thrown out through the meshes of the net, before they are free, after a confinement of a day and a half at the least, so that the great facts stand out for all students of city life to see :—

BRUTALITY AND SULLEN DEFIANCE

are added to and engrafted on the pauper character. With the sullen endurance of the North American Indian they meet their fate; gentler treatment not repelling, and harsh treatment only embittering and degrading.

When the pauperism of a vast city is sunk in sullen despair and degraded life is no longer abhorrent to its victims, and brutality sinks men into savages, so that despair, degradation and brutality become the dominant traits of character of a great pauper mass, then, in the name of God, society has got to put forth mightier energies in more judicious array than heretofore, or fail in its attempt.

I declare before this great audience representing the best civilization of many countries, that

THE METHODS OF DEALING WITH PAUPERISM
HITHERTO APPLIED

are impotent against this swelling tide of brutal degraded pauperism.

England's great Poor Law Reform of 1834 is always cited first. The fundamental principle of this reform was "THAT THE SITUATION OF THE PERSON RECEIVING RELIEF SHOULD NOT ON THE WHOLE BE MADE REALLY OR APPARENTLY SO ELIGIBLE AS THE SITUATION OF THE INDEPENDENT LABORER OF THE LOWEST CLASS." (Nicholl's History of English Poor Law, Vol. 2, p. 257.)

This principle has been everywhere accepted.

Seth Low cites it in his famous attack on the evils of "Out-Door Relief," (1879, p. 3,) as an accepted principle.

The Charity Organization Society of London and of all other cities concur.

In fact the soundness of this principle is unquestioned. The lot of the pauper must not be made too attractive. Yet I am led to ask whether Repression has not been guilty of a fatal error. Has not the system been left to such mere officialism as to be hard and depressing and at last brutalizing?

And this in two directions. First, to the worthy poor, so that all England is now vibrating in recoil from the sad lot of the old and worthy and suffering poor. Second, to the idle, the dissolute, the loafer and the tramp — the unworthy poor.

Do not present conditions in London and New York force us to face a new and graver problem? Yes, and the conditions in cities of the second rank also.

Do not the new race of brutally degraded paupers laugh to scorn the principle of the English Reform of 1834, that their lot shall not be made too attractive? Do they not defy differences of detail of poor law administration? Must we not reckon with the fact that they have resolved only upon one sure and certain thing,

THAT THEY WILL NOT LIVE BY LABOR?

For proof I cite that malignant talisman the story of the Jukes. If any have not read Dugdale's story, let them straightway do so, and see how the mere principle of repression, as society has applied it, in almshouse or jail or by denial of out-relief, failed to prevent a numerous and degraded offspring through many generations enjoying life in every imaginable form of degradation.

Or who can forget that similar story of horrors, "The Social Degradation" of the "Tribe of Ishmael" by Oscar C. McCulloch, five years ago, which will long endure as a powerful argument for speedy and radical reform, to which he gave the wisdom and enthusiasm and organizing energy of his noble life?

If you love statistics, count the number of applicants for relief in the great cities of this land or of England or Germany. Count the convicts annually sent to jail. How many are old repeaters? Can many cities surpass Boston in its list of offenders sent down to the House of Industry two or three or four or five score of times, till the leader of the throng is found perhaps boasting of his one hundred and forty sentences?

What a parody on punishment when the drunken ruffian whom I knew in the South Cove comes home from jail so reckless that he takes from Johnnie's feet the new boots his wife has bought, and the calico gown off his little daughter, to sell for rum, and so degraded that he likes the " Island" as well as his home.*

No wonder Gov. Altgeld of Illinois in his welcome through a friend to the Prison Commission last week said arrests were too many, 70,000 a year in Chicago. Expand this mere statistic to its full meaning. The length and breadth of its lessons are too tremendous.

Has not the principle of repression miserably failed, when its effort to make the lot of the pauper not over eligible hardens tramps into such brutal degradation that in their game with Society they seem just now to hold in their hands the winning cards, and yet on the other hand the worthy poor of England are in such straits, that a great pension scheme throws its baleful shadow across the land? No doubt the conditions of labor there are less favorable than in the United States, wages lower and demand for labor slack, the army of Londoners unemployed increasing, and the lot of worthy poor in their old age appealing to every sympathy.

Do not misunderstand me. I do not object to repression, but to its failure. Why has it failed? Partly no doubt because the whole system of punishment by fine and by brief terms of confinement has failed to be deterrent. Sentimentality has also refused to permit punishment to be reasonably severe.

But the chief reason is that officialism has lacked the humane element absolutely necessary to save its influence from being mechanical and degrading.

---

*" There are soft-hearted persons who would cry out in the name of philanthropy against indeterminate and cumulative sentences, and still more against the incarceration for life of vagabonds who have never done anything worse than go on in beggary, dirt, and drunkenness, and beget children doomed by their birth to idiocy, profligacy, or crime. Yet the sterilization of the unfit by life-long segregation is demanded in the interests of every hope of social morality, and it is a blot upon our civilization that men and women should be sent to the Island or the Bridewell, a dozen times a year for ten days or two weeks at a time, year in, year out, from their first commitment for drunkenness at eighteen or nineteen years of age, till they stumble at last into a pauper's grave. What a senseless mockery of corrective discipline to suppose that a drunkard of forty years' standing is going to be reformed by giving him ten days at the Island for the hundredth time !"—Father J. O. S. Huntington, in Social Progress, p. 186.

Officialism without humanity can punish, but it only sinks the sufferer into worse debasement.

When also punishment ceases to prevent crimes, the problem assumes the most terrible aspect.

How such pauper criminals and criminal paupers can be restored to manhood, is so hard a question that theology sometimes fears it may be beyond the power of God.

No wonder that it is a supreme task for man. Yet this is the exact task which Scientific Charity now has got to accept,—to deal fittingly with degraded need. Sympathy loves to aid the tender and attractive child. It hastens to the side of a widow in her woe. It cares for the sick or the suffering, for victims of fire flood or other casuality, but it has not yet begun to do its duty to the pauper, and too often recoils with horror from that compound of pauperism and vice which is the worst phase of great city life.

REPRESSION ALONE IS A FAILURE.

Charitable work has two sides, the positive and constructive, and the negative or repressive.

The last is content to prevent overlapping, stop begging, discover imposture, cut off needless alms and reduce excessive outdoor relief.

The first aims at improving the condition of a family in any possible wise way, health, home, skill, work, trade, temperance, thrift, cheer, by personal influence, by organizations like Stamp Savings, or the Bedford Industrial Building, or by whatever other wise ways ingenuity can discover. This charity I will call constructive, and the other repressive. Who will not agree with me that

REPRESSIVE CHARITY ALONE

is hard, and that negative measures alone will fail? Only as Charity learns to diagnose and discriminate, and then brings ingenuity to the various problems, with deep and genuine sympathy, boldly summoning to this imperative duty the social and Christian powers of all good men and women in personal service, only so can charity succeed.

The height of this ideal for great cities, I know too well to seek to belittle. Only by stating it in its utmost demands can the mighty powers, as yet dormant or little aroused, of great cities be stirred to their tremendous task. Little cities delight in this duty, and can do it with a measure of success full of inspiration for us all.

NEWPORT

offers a picture of beautiful and devoted work, which I have always delighted to honor and to cite as encouraging proof of what will follow from thorough, patient, persistent, personal work, wisely guided and well done in a small community, where the right influences may be applied in each different case.

Their C. O. S. report in 1880, shows the exact change and improvement in the condition of 220 families, classified at the beginning and at the end of their first year's work.*

Success in Newport has continued. It is largely due to the devotion and wisdom of a few leaders who threw themselves into the new work, and to faithful friendly visiting.

FRIENDLY VISITING.

Cities of the first size like London, New York, Chicago and Philadelphia, differ in no more important respect from smaller

---

*"The amount of out-door relief given by the city for the year 1879-80 was about $2,500 less than the previous year. This was partly due to the fact that the winter was an open one, and out-door work was carried on to an unusual extent. For the current year, 1880-81, the appropriation for the Poor Department has been reduced by $2,000. Up to December first there have been less than one-third as many applicants for relief as there were up to the same date in 1879.

Last year we dwelt chiefly on the necessity for the work, the need of investigation, the duty of withholding indiscriminate alms: this year we show you as the result of those principles, put in practice through some difficulties, that the worthy poor are well cared for; that homes have been bettered, characters improved, the unworthy and disabling spirit of pauperism checked, and above all, that *thrift*, one of the first duties of a citizen, is being taught, if slowly, yet surely."

cities than in their apparent inability to create and maintain " friendly visiting," on any large scale.*

This great topic will be worthily treated tomorrow. Enough here to say that this spirit underlies the best efforts to improve the conditions of the poor, whether en masse, or more especially in their individual needs in many other cities from Brooklyn and Boston down.

With absolute candor I must say that in my judgment where cities are too large for personal relations of friendly sympathy and help — where distances are too great or absorption in the whirl of other cares is too intense, the chasm between the happy and the wretched must go on growing more deep and terrible till the condition of the pauper criminal mass becomes intolerable.

CHICAGO

in this season of her glory, can she pardon critics who suggest that the star of friendly visiting is needed to make her diadem complete?

PHILADELPHIA

began with a goodly corps of friendly visitors but has failed to maintain their efficiency or numbers.

NEW YORK

has not yet conceived it possible to obtain friendly visitors in large numbers.

Read in Hon. A. S. Hewitt's admirable address at the opening of the United Charities Building in New York these words of the Charity Organization Society : — " Its mission is by investigation and registration to guard the public against the abuse of benevo-

---

*"What," says Miss Hill, speaking of the Charity Organization Society, " Is its living call to us all? to come ourselves and help. In every Metropolitan district is its group of workers, men and women of every kind united in but one thought—how to help in wisest and most patient ways every case of want and suffering. Its remedy is the eternal remedy of patient care and thought and wisdom, brought to bear on men and women and children in their own homes by their neighbors. Money, yes, certainly, and *plenty* of it; but abiding and large gifts as citizens for fellow-citizens, sown like separate seeds with care, watched and watched over and given with ourselves to the real service of those we know and love."

lence and to devise and institute measures of prevention, in which reside the only solid hope of a permanent moral improvement."

Whereby it appears that gathering and using a large number of friendly visitors is not alluded to as any part of the New York conception of organized charity.

LONDON.

We read in the Charity Organization Review (July 1893, P. 46) in an article perhaps written by Mr. Loch entitled "American View of Charity Organization Society Work:"

"The second institution to which we should like to refer as evidently held in high estimation by many leading Charity Organization Society thinkers is that of Friendly Visitors.

"How, in America, they manage to obtain qualified friendly visitors on a large scale we do not know.

"The World's Fair at Chicago will give any who wish the opportunity of noting the enthusiasm and hopefulness of the American Societies at first hand."

BOSTON

is perhaps the city where friendly visiting first became an essential part of the new Charity. It formed no part of the original movement in London in 1869. It had been done in Boston on a small scale in ward seven, by the Co-operative Society of visitors before the organization of the Associated Charities, but that body first made formal and definite announcement that friendly visiting would be seriously undertaken in a large way.*

"The great work for friendly visitors" was here explained and developed substantially upon the same lines that it has followed to the present time.

The principle was thus stated in my address at the Social Science Conference, at Saratoga, in September 1880. ("Not Alms, but a Friend." No. 17.)

"Whenever any family has fallen so low as to need relief, send to them at least one friend,—a patient, true, sympathizing, firm friend,—to do for them all that a friend can do to discover and remove the causes of their dependence, and to help them up into independent self-support and self-respect."

---

*(See inaugural address of Robert Treat Paine, March 12, 1879, when chosen President of the Associated Charities of Boston, "Charity Organization," No. 6, Publications of Boston Associated Charities.)

Let me call attention to one fact. The original draft of the Boston Society authorized giving relief if it could be procured from no other source. But this clause was stricken out owing to the opposition of relief societies and as it seems to me by the the finger of God. Visitors were compelled to devote their thought and sympathy in other directions, so admirably described by Miss Octavia Hill, with whatever measure of success has been attained.

Fourteen years' experience justifies more strongly with each new year's results the encouraging claim that in almost every case a friendly visitor can learn how to help and can often succeed in helping into independence a family in distress if he, or usually she, goes into their home and learns the truth; going there not to give alms, but prohibited usually from giving alms, and therefore forced to study how to aid the family in permanent ways.

Statistics year after year show in how many varied ways real help has been given.

BROOKLYN

is the largest city which has successfully developed and maintained efficiently the work of friendly visiting. See Report of Brooklyn Bureau of Charities for 1892, p. 16, for an interesting organization of their visitors for study as a class, and an admirable statement of the

DUTIES OF FRIENDLY VISITORS.

ART. 9, SECT. 2 OF BY-LAWS.

" It shall be the duty of a Friendly Visitor to visit the poor and distressed as a friend ; to examine, in the spirit of kindness, the causes of their trouble; to do what can be done to remove those causes; to become acquainted with the ability which each may have, and to aid in developing it and in finding ways in which it may be employed in self-help; through friendly intercourse, sympathy and direction, to encourage self-dependence, industry and thrift; to recommend whatever may be possible and wise to alleviate the sufferings of those whose infirmities cannot be cured or removed; if material aid be necessary, to obtain it from existing organizations as far as possible; and in every case to promote in all practicable ways the physical and moral improvement of the families in the visitor's charge."

Mr. Alfred T. White, President of the Brooklyn Bureau of Charities, has recently described the excellent work done in that great city. (" The Friendly Visitor's Opportunity," Charities Review, April, 1893, p. 329.)

"It may appear," he says, "a slow process to eliminate poverty piece by piece from our great cities, and it is natural to long for some quicker way, but *there is no way which does not reach to and touch the character of the individual poor.* . . . Surely there never was a time when so many were interested in the elevation of those less favored than themselves."

"Where is the call so clear to us in city life as this need of our neighbors for our personal consideration and service, a need doubly commanding since the organization of charity has so greatly increased the possibilities of successful interest and effort?" (P. 331.)

Here in Mr. White's words is the supreme aim and need of friendly visiting: to "touch the character of the individual poor."

RADICAL REMEDIES.

What reply has Scientific Charity to the question whether the grand aggregate of degraded pauperism in great cities is to increase or decrease, when the forces that work for evil are all weighed :—

The unemployed, an army in London, numerous in New York, not many usually in smaller cities ;—

The inefficient, always in all cities a great number vibrating between work and idleness ;—

Paupers, resolved only on one thing, that they hate work ;—

The terrible element of vice, and the great army of criminals, who war upon Society, not deterred by present penalties ;—

Then add the causes of sickness and low vitality ;—

In some cities all these evils aggregated into great masses.

Simply and surely this first, that merely to deal, no matter how wisely, with single cases of distress or crime as they arise, is infinitely insufficient.

Nay, worse, Prof. W. G. Tucker in his Phi Beta Oration at Harvard, last June, compels us to seek more radical cure, by more radical measures, when he says: "THE PHILANTHROPY WHICH IS CONTENT TO RELIEVE THE SUFFERER FROM WRONG SOCIAL CONDITIONS, POSTPONES THE PHILANTHROPY WHICH IS DETERMINED, AT ANY COST, TO RIGHT THOSE CONDITIONS."

"Who does not know," says Professor H. C. Adams, "that much of our so-called philanthropy *tends to perpetuate those conditions* which seem to make philanthropy necessary? Father

Huntington has rendered a marked service in the strong protest which he urges against the charities of our day. He shows to the discerning mind, that a philanthropy which is satisfied when the cry of the sufferer is hushed, has no place among the permanent forces of social progress." (Social Progress, p. x.)

This brings me to the main purpose of my paper. Has not the new charity organization movement too long been content to aim at a system to relieve or even uplift judiciously single cases without asking if there are not prolific causes permanently at work to create want, vice, crime, disease and death; and whether these causes may not be wholly or in large degree eradicated?

If such causes of pauperism exist, how vain to waste our energies on single cases of relief, when society should rather aim at removing the prolific sources of all the woe.

THE FOUR GREAT CAUSES OF PAUPERISM AND OF DEGRADED CITY LIFE HAVE LONG SEEMED TO ME TO BE THESE:—
1. FOUL HOMES.
2. INTOXICATING DRINK.
3. NEGLECT OF CHILD LIFE.
4. INDISCRIMINATE ALMS GIVING.

Who can closely study the conditions of life among the poor of cities without seeing these malignant forces working day and night to create all forms of degraded life?

Who then will not agree with me that resolute and heroic measures must be taken in all large cities, before conditions become hopeless?

What happier augury can come from this conference than the conviction that all the forces of Scientific and Christian Charity must combine to extirpate these outrages upon the virtue, health and happiness of the masses of the people?

Charles Booth* counts up twenty-three principal causes of pauperism:

Crime, vice, drink, laziness, pauper association, heredity, mental disease, temper, incapacity, early marriage, large family, extravagance, lack of work, trade misfortune, restlessness, no

---

*(" Pauperism and the Endowment of Old Age," p. 9.)

relations, death of husband, desertion, death of father or mother, sickness, accident, ill luck, old age.

But may not all these twenty-three causes, except old age, accident and death, come from wretched life in a foul home, or drunkenness, or neglect when the victim was a child, or indiscriminate giving of alms?

Yes, these four causes are the primary, potent and prolific sources of the degraded life in cities. All of them are remediable in different ways and to different degrees.

How long will it be possible for the public to witness these outrages against itself and against the welfare and the rights of our poorer citizens, without such indignant wrath as to cleanse them away from city life?

FOUL HOMES.

Which of the two causes dragging down the conditions of life among the masses, foul homes or intoxicating drink, is more potent, I do not know. Each leads surely to the other.

Everywhere the conviction gains ground that it is impossible to elevate the conditions of the lower class of working people above the condition of their homes. If they are left in foul and overcrowded slums or damp basements or dilapidated barracks, it is too much to expect them to be virtuous or self-respecting or independent. These rotten slums are hot-beds which propagate low life, shattering the health of occupants and so promoting pauperism, loosening the morals and so promoting vice and crime; and perhaps worst of all in their poisonous influence on the children who grow up in them too often without virtue, self-respect, health or hope.

We all rejoice to see that the increasing interest of Society in the homes of the people is taking shape in many efficient ways.

What I believe to be of great importance to this cause, is that its close relations to the whole pauper problem of great cities should be recognized; so that all observers may see and know that the two causes are only one cause; and the friends of each may see the larger relations of their work and gain power and motive from this consciousness that they are not merely dealing with details, but rather are shaping the conditions of the present and future welfare of the people.

If the aim of all charitable work among the poor is a general improvement of their condition, so the aim of all who are interested in their homes must be to

ESTABLISH A HIGHER STANDARD OF HABITABILITY.

Grand impulse has been given to this movement in England by four persons, Lord Shaftesbury, Octavia Hill, Sir Sydney Waterlow and George Peabody.

Lord Shaftesbury began the movement to improve the homes of working people in 1842, of which time he says: " So little were people acquainted with the state of the houses in which laboring people dwelt, that we treated the question as an entirely new one. Many persons then thought that we were undertaking a quixotic work, and that there was really very little that required amendment. But I am happy to say that the improvement of the condition of the working classes in a domiciliary aspect is now almost a trite subject."

He was the first witness before the Royal Commission of 1884 and his words describing the horrors of the abodes of the poor shocked all England. When he died in 1886, full of honors and beloved of all, he had no juster claim to honor and love than his life-long services for the homes of plain people.

Octavia Hill came next in order of time but she stands supreme thus far in the world's history among and above all others who have thought, labored and lived for and among the poor, to improve their homes.

Octavia Hill and Sir Sydney Waterlow are entitled to rank among the great discovers of this world, now that Sociology takes its due rank, above all natural sciences, next only to the knowledge of God.

Miss Hill discovered and has taught the world the true relations of landlord and tenant. She has created a Normal school in this art. Men and women from this country as well as England try to learn the sweet and beautiful and wonderfully potent, uplifting influence which she and her band of rent collectors have been exerting for years among the very humblest classes of tenants in some of the gloomiest courts of London. Let Sociologists watch the spread of this new power through the world, and teach it to every school.

Sir Sydney Waterlow's discovery ranks next in value to workingmen. Risking first his own means alone, he learned and proved that even in a great city like London, where land values are high, model tenement houses, built with all reasonable conveniences and comforts, can be made a commercial success. This discovery introduces into modern civilization a potent force to improve the homes of the people. Its effect has been so powerful as to have changed the face of London. Capital has been attracted by the millions of pounds sterling; one company alone of which Sir Sydney is President, "The Improved Industrial Dwellings Co." has built thirty blocks in different parts of London at a cost of $5,000,000, and offers to some 30,000 souls homes not devoid of aesthetic charm, at moderate rents, which yield five per cent. on the capital.

Alfred T. White has achieved a like success with Model Blocks in Brooklyn, on a large scale.*

The Boston Coöperative Building Company has in 22 years provided 76 houses, with 962 rooms, for 325 families, at a cost of $400,000 in Boston. These tenements are eagerly sought by intelligent tenants, and the investment has been most successful in all respects.

THREE AGENCIES

directly deal with the task of fitly housing the people:

1. Philanthropic Agencies which aim to improve the condition both of tenants and of the tenements they occupy.

2. Economic Agencies providing decent homes, often in model buildings.

3. Municipal Agencies aiming to abolish the worst evils and to destroy foul homes.

High above each and all of these three agencies in its influence and promise of grand results, I place the rising ambition of workingmen themselves to own their own homes. †

---

* Described in his " Improved Dwellings for the Laboring Classes," 1879, and " Better Homes for Workingmen," 1885, Conference of Charities.

† H. M. Hyndman of the Social Democratic Federation, addressing the Labor Commission in England, objects to thrift in Workingmen, because it only makes them small capitalists, buttressing the class they should supplant and intensifying the competition from which they suffer!—[Econ. Journal, March, 1893, p. 169.]

If this laudable ambition is lacking among the lowest class, so also do both of the powerful agencies at work to provide model homes, whether by philanthropic or invested capital of which I have just spoken, shoot over their heads.

The agency which must be invoked to rescue the very poor, whether virtuous and struggling, or degraded and indifferent, is *the municipal power to destroy utterly unfit abodes of habitations.*

Sad, indeed, is the fact that when charity aids some wretched family to move out of a vile basement or dark and nasty slum, presently some other like family moves in.

The growth of public sentiment towards practical unanimity in this decision has been marked by important measures in London, Glasgow and other cities of Great Britain.

The London Charity Organization Society Reports on the Dwellings of the Poor record this progress. (1873 and 1881.)

I will only quote here the judgment of one man, which has aided in this enlightened movement.

Dr. Gairdner, Medical Officer of Health for Glasgow, wrote: " I believe that nuisance removal, epidemic inspection, cleansing, ventilating, and suppression of over-crowding, are all good up to a certain point. . . . *But in relation to the persistent and slowly-accumulating evils of our great towns, the social rottenness, so to speak, that is in them all, these are mere surface-measures. . . . . I am putting it roundly, perhaps you will even say paradoxically, but I am stating the result of a deep conviction, when I say that the destructive part of the duty of the authorities is of more importance, if possible, than the constructive; that the first and more essential step is to get rid of the existing haunts of moral and physical degradation." ***

This movement to destroy the slums is under powerful headway.

Rome, Paris, London, Glasgow, New York and Boston, and so on in different degree, have all set to work to exterminate those rotten spots or foul abodes which tainted human life.

I place this movement at the head as the most powerful force conducing to improve the condition of the abject poor.

How it can be made more thoroughly effective, is the most important question I may send home with each of my hearers.

---

* Report of the Dwellings Committee of the Charity Organization Society, 1873, p. 9.

Pass in review our co-workers and then let us see how they can be strengthened.

The medical profession to a man, economists, ministers and churches, philanthropists and workers among the poor, novelists and the press, and last and most efficacious, Boards of Health.

New York gave a powerful impulse by the investigation and report of the Board of Health in 1887.

Boston did the same by the Report of Professor Dwight Porter in 1889, and Gen. F. A. Walker, whose judgment carries weight not surpassed in the United States, at the meeting where this report was presented, stated : —

"I believe that a true view of the economy of State action may not infrequently disclose the occasion for saving a great deal of interference and a great deal of State action, in subsequent stages, by putting the firm hand of government upon the very sources of evil, and applying the powers of the State to crush out social mischief in its inception. I confess that it has for some time seemed to me increasingly probable that the social philosophy of the age would soon come to recognize the Housing of the Very Poor as *the* point at which the remedial action of the Government may be applied, not only with the highest effect upon the happiness and health of the community, but actually with large resulting reductions from the sum of State action and governmental authority.

It would be an act, either of monstrous ignorance or of monstrous impudence on the part of any man, contemplating the changes of public sentiment which have taken place on this subject within the last fifteen, ten and five years, to put his foot down and say, 'thus far and no farther will I go towards enlarging the functions of the State.' In view of the great developments of the immediate past, the most likely thing in regard to each one of us by turns, is that, in five, ten, or fifteen years from now, he will be occupying a position on this subject very different from that he now anticipates. Yet I confess I have of late been coming rapidly to the conviction that ere long there will be a general consent of conservative citizens, in every enlightened State, to regard as thoroughly good politics all interference by law which may be necessary to prevent any portion of the people from living in houses which are unfit for human habitation, residence in which is incompatible with health or with social or personal decency.

I expect soon to see the time come when the Commonwealth of Massachusetts shall declare that no one of its citizens, under whatever plea of poverty, shall have his home where he has not a sufficient access of fresh air and of God's sunlight, and where the conditions as to drainage and the disposal of refuse are not such as to afford reasonable security for the health of the individual, and to protect society against communicable disease. I believe that not only will the law of the Commonwealth say this, which, indeed, is little more than it now says, but that the public sentiment of the community will have been so educated on this subject as to support the officers of the law in whatever rigorous and painful measures may be required for the thorough, systematic and unrelenting enforcement of the most advanced sanitary requirements."

DESTROY THE SLUMS.

No movement can be inaugurated in any city, more potent to improve the conditions of the most wretched poor and to cut off the supply of degraded pauperism, than the movement to destroy the slums.

Probably no city has been wholly inactive. But I am sure no large city in this country has begun to act up to the standard required for the health or morals of the poor, or by economy to the public, or by principles of justice and right.

Boards of Health have power probably in all cities to vacate dwellings unfit for human habitation. All that is needed is *Aroused Public Interest* to learn the unspeakable horrors of the homes of the wretched poor today, and then to insist on a *Higher Standard of Habitability.*

Boards of Health will follow the public command and the public conscience.

Boston is taking active steps in this direction. A number of public-spirited men and women have organized a "Better Dwellings Society," which has directed attention to many intolerable rotten spots. The Board of Health is acting with judicious firmness in vacating unfit homes below an accepted standard, which has been steadily rising for a score of years in compliance with enlightened public judgment.

Yet Boston has many terrible abodes of vice and wretchedness still left where all circumstances concur for evil life.

It is a cause of surprise and regret to find in the reports of Charity Organization or Relieving Societies of different cities so little attention paid to this supreme yet eradicable cause of pauperism and crime.*

New York finds this problem of housing the poor more difficult than any other city of the world. The Report of "The Association for Improving the Condition of the Poor " (1892, p. 60), describes their action as to homes of the poor, viz. :

---

*Nor any allusion to it in that superb history by Mr. Kellogg last evening of all the C. O. S. work for these twenty years.

516 inspections,
251 reports to the Board of Health,
760 causes for complaints,¦and of these
76 were for filthy premises,
54 were for dirty yards,
27 were for wet cellars.

Yet the surprising thing is that only thirty complaints seem to point at radical evils. "Buildings generally dilapidated." Even here action hardly seems to be aimed at, of *wholly vacating* the buildings as fatally and hopelessly unfit.

The Pittsburg Report of "The Association for Improving the Condition of the Poor" (1892, p. 8) states that visitors made 20,915 visits to the poor, visiting "homes in basements that are *unhealthy through dampness and no sunshine* and to people who live in old boats." Yet no fierce protests of righteous indignation are made to Boards of Health.

Chicago will, I hope, permit a few frank words about this terrible source of pauperism.

The Report for 1892, (p.   ) of the "Chicago Relief Society," states :

"The general circumstances and conditions of the poor in Chicago are much more favorable than in most large cities in this or any other country. The proportion of paupers is much less. Most of the working class in Chicago live in their little cottages, in many cases owned by their occupants, or in comfortable rooms in houses usually occupied by two or three families and seldom by more than four or five, at rents from $5 to $7 monthly."

Yet on the other hand, the last Report I have seen of the "United Hebrew Relief Society" of Chicago states, (1885–86) under the heading of "Tenement Houses for the Poor" :

"*Sickness has been deplorably prevalent. The evil may be traced to the unwholesome habitations in which the poor generally reside.* These dwellings not only destroy physical vigor, but they stifle the mind and blunt the morals. They are inimical to the cause of education as they are dangerous to bodily health."*

---

*On June 8, 1893, I visited some of the wretched abodes of the very poor in Chicago with an officer kindly detailed by Chief of Police Mr. McClaughry. The sights were too sad for words. One cellar was so poisoned with sewer gas and the effluvia of leaking water closets that the tenant said, in not wholly crushed despair, "I have lost one child here and don't propose to lose another," (No. 359 Clarke Street). Another utterly dilapidated barrack, (543 Clarke Street) about 30x90 feet, swarming with Italian children from eight to ten families, has long been utterly unfit for human beings to live in.

As you ride out to the World's Fair to see the latest triumph of architecture and art in these days, look down from the South Side Elevated Railroad (the Alley road, so-called) near the 21st Street Station on the West, or again at 26th Street, at the wretched slums below you. The protracted picture of conditions of intolerable life points my argument that the problem of poor relief in great cities knows no possible solution till these hot-beds which propagate degraded pauper life are absolutely abolished.

Would to God my words could strengthen the conviction of every delegate to this Congress, as he goes home to his own city, that slums must be abolished.

So might public interest be more keenly aroused and the good cause gain momentum, as one city after another joined in judicious and resolute action.

INTOXICATING DRINK

is the second great cause of pauperism, crime and many other wretched conditions of degraded life.

The Temperance Reform makes perceptible headway although the most powerful passions of mankind oppose its progress. In the last ten years, England has seen a great improvement in the conditions of the working people in this respect.

In the United States prohibition or high license or restricted license, or the Gottenburg system, or that new state system in South Carolina, or local option which secures no license in many cities and towns, all these movements mark a great popular awakening to the terrible influence of drunkenness upon the welfare of the people.

Their improved conditions where temperance prevails are so evident, that for instance in Massachusetts the smaller cities are making steady progress in the direction of voting for no license in the annual struggle. The contest in such states as Iowa and Kansas marks the growing popular condemnation of the evil. In spite of all this progress, more or less visible throughout the civilized world, the gigantic power of the rum shop to drag its victims down rages through the world with insolent defiance of the sympathy and intelligence of good citizens to discover and execute any efficient method of suppression.

My object here is to propose and stimulate an alliance of these two forces, the friends of temperance and all the other forces working to improve the conditions of the poor. Such an alliance will strengthen both and lead each party to see the broader scope of their task.

NEGLECT OF CHILDREN.

The third prolific cause of pauperism is found in the conditions of neglect or maltreatment of child life in great cities.*

Two specifications of the boys' indictment against society have been mentioned. Absence of play-grounds almost compels him to choose, in a great city, between stupidity and crime. Absence of manual training forces him to live by his wits or by commonest forms of labor.† But I wish especially to draw attention to the need of a great development of charity in the treatment of widows with young children.

Large cities are disputing about the comparative merits of systems, all of which are so unworthy of our age, and so cruel to the mother and dangerous to the welfare of the child that the time has come for worthier treatment by the best method science and sympathy can devise.

No one will deny the influence growing out of different systems of dealing with this class of children. The systems in England,

---

*Hon. A. S. Hewitt in his address at the opening of the United Charities Building of New York, (*Charities Review*, April, 1893, p. 304,) says:—" In this city a large number of children of both sexes live in an atmosphere of poverty and vice, and even crime, which educates them to be paupers and criminals instead of training them to become honest workmen and good citizens. And for this result, which is generally no fault of their own, they are punished, and, along with them, the industrious class of the community is also punished by taxation for the support of poorhouses, hospitals and criminals. Gangs of young men not yet twenty-one years of age are to be found in many parts of the city, who, not having been permitted to learn trades, or having been denied the opportunity to follow some useful occupation, have grown up in idleness, and expend their animal energies in excesses which make them a terror to the neighborhood and a trial to the police, the only barrier between them and crime. In time most of them necessarily become criminals and they are very sure to breed criminals. The public is not dealing with this great menace to society either with sense or firmness."

†Which alcoves in all the vast and varied World's Fair are richer in promise for the welfare of the coming generation of men than the alcoves full of the results of manual training in many cities?

New York, and Massachusetts are radically different. No one of them can escape condemnation.

England very largely refuses out-relief to the widow with children, breaks up the family, and sends one or more of the children into the district school or into that department of the almshouse called the Industrial School, usually a vast institution where children are gathered by hundreds. The mother is left with only one or two children whom she may be able to support.

Am I wrong in ranking the English system as least favorable for the happiness of the home or the future welfare of the child, unjust to both mother and child, and not worthy of the Christian philanthropy of the age?*

The New York system has no provision of out-door relief for such a family of children, and resembles the English method in that the family must be broken up, but the children instead of being sent to great public institutions, are distributed among private institutions which receive a per capita allowance from the state; tempting them to promote this destruction of family life.

This method seems to me next to merit condemnation because it allows money consideration to break up families, even where a worthy mother is struggling to preserve her child and her home, and because secondly these children are condemned to institution life and as yet as Mrs. Lowell of New York says †"It is to be remembered that the poorest home, unless it be a degraded one, is better than any institution."

---

*Quest. 5838.—What system would you like to see substituted?

Mrs. Charles.—"I should like to see boarding-out as far as possible, and the plan of taking children from their mothers and sending them to a district school, by way of giving them poor relief, I think is a mistake. It would be far better, in my opinion, I having had very considerable experience, to give the poor widows a little out-door relief, and allow them to keep their children at home. It acts in this way also upon the mothers. They find that they can part with their children, and throw off their responsibilities; and it is not right for anyone to be allowed to throw off the responsibility she has voluntarily incurred. That is another evil of the district school system, that Poor Law guardians will give widows relief in the shape of sending their children to these schools, then the widows are free, and I am sorry to say I have known many instances where the widows have not conducted themselves as well as they would have done if they had had the responsibility of their children at home."—Report House of Lords Com., Poor Law Relief, Aug. '88, p. 641.

(†" Public Relief and Private Charity," p. 74.)

Mrs. Lowell brings this further charge, "that unfortunately in New York City at least, the custom has grown up of requiring that judges shall commit children to private institutions, as a necessary condition of obtaining payment from the city for their support. This undoubtedly is a dangerous proceeding, since the familiarization with a court of law tends to destroy the dread of arrest, which should be fostered as one of the strongest deterrent influences against crime. To bring a child before a judge in a criminal court in order to secure his entrance into an institution of charity is a most unwise measure."

The dependent child problem has attained great proportions in New York City where 15,697 boys and girls are supported at an annual charge of $1,500,000 out of a population of 1,600,000 in 1889, or a proportion of 1 to 100. While Massachusetts had 1951 dependent children out of 2,000,000 souls, or 1 to 1025, Pennsylvania had 10,000 dependent children, 1 to 450, while Michigan had only 200 dependent children, or 1 to 10,000.*

The Massachusetts system aims to keep families together where there is a not totally unfit home, and if relief is not obtained from some other source, the Overseers of the Poor give, and continue, needed relief to a widow until the children grow to an age when their labor added to their mother's earnings can support the home.†

Many competent judges cannot believe that the Massachusetts system works well for the child, though it is certainly more humane for the mother than the system either in England or New York.

The poisonous influence of our out-door pauper relief must be felt upon the child's character in many cases, yet the family is kept together, and the children are brought up under the loving care and influence of their mother, free from the injurious influence of any institution, and especially escaping the almshouse brand.

Critics who urge the total abolition of out-door relief may claim that this system works badly even in this class of cases, and

---

(*Report State Board of Char. of N. Y., 1890, p. 33.)

†Prof. Francis Wayland in his paper on Out-Door Relief, [1877,] gives the weight of his judgment in favor of Out-Door Relief, especially in "cases where the head of the family is removed by death or prostrated by sickness, and where there is reasonable prospect of the mother being able to keep her family together and ultimately maintain them." (Page 9.)

sometimes with justice when pauper relief leaves upon the child a pauper taint.

Do you ask whether in Massachusetts we think our system the best and are resolved to maintain it? I answer frankly, *No.*

Here is a better method which I believe to be the best. Aid the mother to maintain her home, provide adequate relief, but free from any pauper poison. Let it go from her church, from some private society, from some benevolent individual. Let it go as from the hand of a friend, as the circumstances of each special case may suggest to be best to the friendly visitor who undertakes the continuous task. Shame on the charity of any city which shrinks from this duty.

This is the reform which in the judgment of many of us in Massachusetts, should be engrafted upon our public relief system.

This is the class of cases which has always been used most effectively by our Overseers of the Poor in advocating the necessity of out-door relief. Taking from the Overseers this class of cases would greatly facilitate its total abolition, or great reduction. This is the special reform which I strenuously advocated in the report of the Associated Charities of Boston in 1882, basing my argument upon the analysis of 938 families in the care of one conference, of whom only 370 received aid in 1884-5 or 1885-6. Only 119 of those were aided in the last year by the Overseers of the Poor, and of these only 20 received over $20 each, of whom four were aided because there were children, receiving in all $159.50.*

The result of this analysis was that a few thousand dollars of benevolent funds would replace out-relief to this class of widows and orphans, and provide for them in the best possible way, by judicious aid from a friendly hand, usually not known either to child or neighbor. How long will it be before Charity fully assumes this loving but imperative duty to the widow with her children?

I have not yet exhausted the list of wrongs which boys and girls suffer at the hands of society, often thereby started on a wrong road through life.

Enough if I can show that neglect and maltreatment of the " Child Problem in great cities " is one of the prolific causes of

---

*Boston is in recent years devoting more thought and care to the child problem and with excellent results. See Reports of *Children's Aid Society, North Bennet Street Home,* and *Boys' Institute of Industry.*

pauperism and crime which must be remedied if society is in earnest to improve the conditions of the poor.*

INDISCRIMINATE ALMSGIVING

is the fourth and a most potent cause of pauperism. It has been considered in these conferences from the start. Yet we have much to learn. Charles Lamb is its only defender, who says "give, asking no questions." Fowle states the rule to be "that the amount of pauperism is in proportion to the amount of relief."

Let me avoid the vexed question whether total abolition of public out-door relief is judicious, in order to fasten attention on the principle universally accepted by experts that as lax relief has created pauperism, so adherence by private as well as public relief, especially by the charitable public, to rigid rules, excluding all but those whose need is well founded, has greatly lessened both the number of paupers as well as the cost of relief.†

Brooklyn, with its dramatic and wonderful reform, little Brookline‡ also, and several great English Unions, all teach the same lesson.

---

* In " *Poverty and its Relief in the U. S.*," p. 14, Dr. Ashrott says : "The Societies for organizing Charities took up this movement, and to their inspiration it is due that the number of charitable societies which care for poor, deserted, neglected and exposed children, has increased in a very rapid manner. All America is now covered with a network of so-called Children's Aid Societies. There is scarcely a State in the Union in which there is not at least one such society to be found."

† The Boston Commission of 1878 on the treatment of the poor, declared (page 5) :

" Experience shows that a steady persistence in limiting relief to support in some public institution, where labor is required under reasonable restraint diminishes the amount of out-door relief without any proportional increase of indoor relief. The applicant supports himself, or is provided for by his friends."

But the Committee are not ready to recommend the abolition of out-door relief, but only that rules for its sharp limitation should be rigidly adhered to, and they say (page 8) that the " rules may be relaxed for recent widows with young children."

‡ CONFERENCE OF CHARITIES AND CORRECTIONS, 1891, page 47.

The experience of Brookline shows how effectively an improved system may reduce pauperism.

Mrs. James M. Codman states that out-door relief had amounted to $9,000 for a population of 6,000, and that after careful investigation had somewhat

Yet the recent facts must give us pause.   Rev. S. A. Barnett of St. Jude's, Whitechapel, the head of Toynbee Hall, states that the effort to provide pensions by private charity for the aged worthy poor must be counted a failure; since it is with great difficulty that 100 pensioners in the three East End Missions of London, where out-relief is given up, are provided by appeals through the whole of London.

Again, the conviction that the lot of the poor in England is too hard and their treatment under the poor law too severe has caused such reaction that a Pension Scheme of $85,000,000 a year hangs in the air, and a Royal Commission has been created to consider the condition of the Poor.

Of course the lot of the laborer in England cannot be compared with that in this country.   Still let us beware of any extreme attack upon out-door relief which shall result in violent reaction.

Three reforms of the abuses of out-door relief should receive universal sanction, and will effect in very large measure the end which all parties desire : dealing with the unworthy, those out of work, and the inefficient.

First.   To the unworthy, rigid prohibition of all relief, public or private, so that, abandoning all hope of it, they shall seek their own support.   This includes the lazy, idle, shiftless, extravagant or vicious paupers, as also in most cases those with relatives or friends.

---

reduced the numbers, there were still 355 persons on the list of paupers. After strong opposition, it was decided to build an almshouse, and " notice was then given that in future no rent would be paid for any one, no fuel allowed, no able-bodied man would be helped in any way, and out-door relief would be given only in very exceptional cases."

" Now for the results. Within a year the number of persons relieved fell to 53, no able-bodied man has ever even applied for help, the number at the almshouse has never exceeded seven, and this number was only at the time when the experiment was tried of caring for some of the harmless insane there, an experiment speedily abandoned. While the population of the town has doubled, the amount expended for the relief of the poor is now $6,000, of which $2,500 goes to pay the board of our largely increased number of insane in the State institutions, leaving $3,500 the amount actually expended for the poor; $1,500 for the almshouse, and the balance for out-door relief in our own town, and largely for temporary relief of our poor in other towns and cities. With all this there has been no suffering."

Second. The provision for men or women out of work demands most serious study of ablest economists and statesmen. The magnitude of the problem in London, present and prospective, affrights the imagination. One road leads to danger; permanent municipal industries which would attract the shiftless into larger masses, whereas the only safety lies in scattering them through the community.*

Not of course that they should starve. They must be dealt with as individuals. How great cities like London, Chicago and New York escape the dilemma of cruelty or of indiscriminate alms-giving, without friendly visitors in goodly number, we in Boston do not know.

The third and grand reform aims to recreate the inefficient, always in great cities a numerous class, into self-support by skill and cheer, and to save them from gratuitous relief as deadly poison.† I cannot learn what New York, Chicago or London do with this class except to leave them to struggle with the law that the unfit must perish.

Charles Booth in his brilliant chapter on "The Unemployed," expresses regret that the problems of the working class are often confounded with the

PROBLEMS OF THE INEFFICIENT.

To confound these two problems is to render the solution of both impossible.‡

The problem of poor relief in cities has no department where results are more largely dependent on the most judicious treatment of both science and sympathy.

To the inefficient, when out of work and in need, nothing can be worse than alms and doles, dragging them down into paupers.

---

* Beware however of aiding by alms able-bodied men or women.

† "I consider it the greatest problem in philanthropy to make human beings who are capable of work out of individuals who otherwise must become paupers, and in this way to create useful members of society."—*My Views on Philanthropy, by Baron de Hirsch*, p. 1, No. Am. Rev., July, 1891.

‡ Miss Jane Addams, in Social Progress, page 55.

Nothing can be better than cheer, counsel, and assistance to gain needed skill and courage.

Professor Franklin H. Giddings, in his essay on the Ethics of Social Progress, develops a new law of the Evolution of Society or rather of a new possible slavery with startling power:

" Neither oppression nor greed has been at any time the first cause of legal bondage or of economic dependence. Both are secondary causes, induced by experiences with a slavery already existent.

Modern civilization does not require, it does not even need, the drudgery of needle-women or the crushing toil of men in a score of life-destroying occupations. If these wretched beings should drop out of existence and no others stood ready to fill their places, the economic activities of the world would not greatly suffer. A thousand devices latent in inventive brains would quickly make good any momentary loss. The true view of the facts is that these people continue to exist after the kinds of work that they know how to perform have ceased to be of any considerable value to society. Society continues to employ them for a remuneration not exceeding the cost of getting the work done in some other and perhaps better way.

The economic law here referred to is one that has been too much neglected in scientific discussion. It ought to be repeated and illustrated at every opportunity, for at present it stands in direct contradiction to current prepossessions. We are told incessantly that unskilled labor creates the wealth of the world.

It would be nearer the truth to say that large classes of unskilled labor hardly create their own subsistence. The laborers that have no adaptiveness, that bring no new ideas to their work, that have no suspicion of the next best thing to turn to in an emergency, might be much better identified with the dependent classes than with the wealth-creators. Precisely the same economic law offers the true interpretation of ancient slavery. In strictness civilization did not rest on slavery. It was not in any true sense maintained by slavery. The conditions that created the civilization created economic dependence, and they are working in the same way, with similar results, today.

Ancient civilization accepted the dependence, and utilized it in the crude form of slavery. Modern civilization accepts and utilizes it in the slightly more refined form of the wages system.

Certain great social tasks of creative organization have always confronted our race. The enforced effort to achieve them has been history's great competitive examination. The slaves and serfs have been those who have failed. The first great necessity was social unity,— the power to act together in a disciplined way, — and the first slaves were those who could not create a sufficiently coherent social organization to sustain a growing civilization. They had to make way before others who were equal to that great achievement, and they became slaves not solely nor chiefly because of a conqueror's tyranny, but primarily because slavery or serfdom was practically the only economic disposition that could be made of them. Today social unity has been in good measure established and the world has entered on yet larger undertakings. The condition and assurance of freedom today is the ability to devise new things, to create new opportunities, to make not only two blades of grass grow where one grew before, but to make a hundred kinds of grass grow where before grew only one kind.

Accordingly, the practically unfree task-workers of this present time are those who, unaided, can accomplish none of these new things. They are those who might do well in old familiar ways, but who have nothing to turn to when their ways cease to be of value to the world. To live they must force depreciated services upon society on any terms that society can continue to pay. They are unfree task-workers not because society chooses to oppress them, but because society has not yet devised or stumbled upon any other disposition to make of them. Civilization, therefore, is not cruel. It is ever supporting and trying in many ways to utilize the wrecks and failures of its own imperfect past."

What can withstand this new inroad of slavery, this sinking of the unskilled into social bondage, but a thorough system of

TEACHING SKILL

to the inefficient, supplemented by almost infinite social sympathy for those who fail?

One of the best standards today to test the progress of constructive Christian Charity of the various towns and cities of our own or any country, is to see what practical measures have been devised to convert the inefficient into an efficient worker.

Charity sewing-schools were rather a poor start. Laundries followed, and promise well.

In Boston, Trinity Church has for a dozen years carried on Trinity Laundry to teach skill and provide work, employing about a hundred different women annually, and paying out in wages about $3,500 each year.

Several other agencies are at work also expressly aiming to teach skill in some handiwork to adults who desire this aid, some of whom should rank as inefficient while others may have used well all their opportunities, but are ambitious of further progress.

Then the Wells Memorial Workingmen's Institute has for years offered free evening instruction to journeymen seeking knowledge in their own trades. The class on the steam engine attracts mechanics to the weekly lecture from towns within a radius of 20 miles, while that on electricity given by Prof. Puffer to over a hundred of the journeymen working in all departments of that difficult art, is perhaps the most interesting attempt to aid workingmen to increased skill.

The Cooper Institute in New York, and the Pratt Institute in Brooklyn, train young men before they begin work. So also do Col. Auchmuty's admirable trade schools in New York. The mechanic arts schools of Philadelphia, Baltimore, Boston, St. Louis and Chicago, are full of promise for the increased skill and larger earnings and brighter future of the youth of our land.

Has all of this nothing to do with my subject? Everything to do with it. I will be silent in despair, unless we who want to solve the problem of our cities' poverty can hope to see our whole land tingle with the fixed and intelligent resolve that the boys and the girls as they grow up, shall have, besides such training of the brain in books as they can get and hold, such training also of all the rest of the body, the various senses, especially the eye and the finger, as will fill the land with artistic and skilled mechanics, and so increase the earning powers of labor and open a brighter future for workingmen.

Here then is one great remedy for the evil conditions which create need. The whole standard of manual skill and of cultivated taste must be raised and widely disseminated, so that the children of the working classes shall have a fair chance in the race of life, and not start under such heavy handicap, that they soon fail and despair.

What city will however dare to appeal from my decision that for thorough system for training the inefficient into skill, and inspiring them with new courage for the struggle of life, Brooklyn is entitled to the palm?

The Bedford Industrial Building* just completed at Brooklyn under the guiding inspiration of Mr. G. B. Buzelle, who has just closed a life of exquisite devotion, and of Mr. A. T. White, and by gifts incited by their aid, at a cost of about $40,000, seems to me on the whole the best building ever yet built as a workshop of human character, to lift on to their feet the poor who largely for lack of skill are discouraged and down, and enable them to stand and walk.

* COPY OF LETTER OF A. T. WHITE TO R. T. PAINE, MAY 27, 1893.

" The work of our Bureau of Charities in Brooklyn has been in part the evolution of our surroundings in Brooklyn, part Mr. Buzelle's ten years devoted service, and part and most largely the experience of some of our most capable Friendly Visitors, Committeemen or Trustees, in which together with many others I have had a certain part. Actually the wood yards, laundries and work-rooms in turn were embodiments of suggestions and requests coming back to the Board from our Visitors, and not provided in advance of such.

We have been occupying for five years, as tenants, a building which we fitted up in very much the same way as the new Bedford Building is fitted up, and in which our Central offices, Central Laundry, workrooms, etc., are now located under a twenty years' lease. In the Bedford Building, which we own, we were not able to make a great many changes that seemed to us improvements. The changes we did make are really of minor importance. That tells you better than anything else how satisfied we have been with the plans evolved five years ago. Besides the building which we lease, and the Bedford Building which we own, we need one more building, but shall have to wait some years for it. The three buildings together would give us a triangle with about two miles distance on each side, three centres of work from which we think we could take care of our work in good shape for a good many years to come. We should not change the scheme or plan of the buildings in any way that I can now think of.

As to the general interest in Brooklyn in the Bureau of Charities, I should say it is steadily increasing and in a wholesome fashion, but our supporters are more among the middle and less wealthy classes than among those of the largest means. This is wholesome for the future while it drops the financial burden on a few for the present."

" ON THE FRIENDLY VISITORS' OPPORTUNITY."

CHARITIES REVIEW FOR APRIL, 1893—p. 328.

" Day after day and week after week," writes Alfred T. White, " our friendly visitors came back to us saying, ' This man or this woman says he cannot get work, but would take it if he could. What shall we do?' Today we answer the question in two well-equipped laundries, two large workrooms for unskilled and unrecommended women, and two woodyards for able-bodied men, all under the control of the Brooklyn Bureau of Charities. There the visitor quickly learns whether the applicant really wishes work, and whether he will stick to work if found; and if this be proved, effort is made to secure for him more permanent and remunerative employment. *Some of our visitors are wise enough to recognize that the moment a woman enters the workroom marks a crisis in the life of many an applicant for aid, and as the chemist stands by his crucible and watches for the time when the pure metal may be detached from its impurities, so the friend who stands by in such a crisis of life sees the elements of character slowly separating, and may eliminate some of the baser stuff before this supreme opportunity is lost. Such workrooms without the friendly visitor would be worthless; they would be solely so many shops; but the friendly visitors' work give them a character and influence which can hardly be over-estimated."*

The Bedford Industrial Building seems to me to serve such a useful function in the supremely interesting problem of how to deal with the inefficient, broken down, depressed poor of our great cities, not properly equipped for the struggle of life, that I try thus to attract the utmost attention to its methods and aims.

What city has got its one or more Bedford Industrial Buildings?

What city is there which can do without?

Let me magnify my office for a good purpose, and declare that no city is adequately equipped which has not one or more Industrial Training Buildings to provide training for the inefficient, and while this process is going on, also powerful personal encouragement and cheer from loving friends.

THESE ARE THE CONCLUSIONS

drawn from a study of the sadder side of life in great cities.

The separate problem of poor relief is insoluble.

Pauperism, vice and crime are common factors of the inseparable and tremendous problem how to uplift the general conditions of life among the poor.

First. The difficulties increase in more than geometrical ratio with the masses of congestion no longer of pauperism alone, but of vice and crime and broken health commingled into base and often brutal degradation.

Second. Negative treatment, the mere principle of repression, while just as needed today and always, as when declared in the reform of 1834, not only fails to repel paupers in their lowest

estate, but tends to degrade them into that reckless or brutal in-
difference, so much sadder for them as well as more hopeless for
society, while also it is open to such charge of harshness to the
worthy aged poor, more numerous in England than here, that
English philanthrophy wavers towards a vast scheme of pension-
ing all the aged, good and bad, rich and poor alike, a burden I
fear too tremendous to be borne.

This principle of repression sinks the humane Wayfarers' Lodge
of Boston, or Philadelphia, or as proposed in New York, into the
prison cell of London's casual ward.

Repression alone makes Guardians or Overseers of the Poor,
and all relieving agents, managers of almshouses, jails and
prisons, and especially the police * who guard the city's peace,
hard, cold and unsympathetic, so that the sad multitude who pass
under their influence, grow more brutally defiant.

In short, mere repression is a cruel and unchristian failure.

Third. Therefore, all work among the poor and wretched,
whether done by official agents, or police, or friendly visitors
whose name should be legion, all efforts to keep families unbroken
and children near to the love of a widowed mother, all efforts to
train and cheer the inefficient must be permeated, energized,
ennobled by the mighty force of love ;—

Love which Drummond shows to be the Greatest Thing in the
World, in that burst of inspiration which everyone should read ;—

Love, described by St. Paul in one of the three noblest chapters
of all human literature ;—

Love, which so moved the soul of God, that He sent His Son
to our rescue ;—

Love, not in weak sentiment, but strengthened by all the vig-
orous firmness of strong men, so that repression may be resolute ;
yet conscious Love shall permeate every fibre of the force which
would hope to deal successfully with the pauper, the criminal or
the brute.

---

* "Moreover, there are few persons in the community more deserving of
the sympathy and support of good people than an honest policeman located
in a bad city quarter. He has to stem the tide of the city's moral defilement,
as no other person is called upon to do; and he is almost wholly deprived of
the uplift, which nearly every social worker now feels, that comes from
knowing of a great body of true men and women who are glad of the work
he is doing."

Love is the motive to summon hundreds of Friendly Visitors from their sunny homes, to go down into the wretched abodes of gloom, where the battle of civilization is to be lost or won, ready to act up to their motto of "Not Alms but a Friend,"*and seeking a fuller measure of ingenuity, discrimination, and patience than Boston has learned, guided by the lesson of encouraging success described by Alfred T. White in Brooklyn, inspired by the life work and words of wisdom of Octavia Hill in London, till this spirit shall recreate the relations of the wretched and the happy; and the superb energies of philanthropy in New York shall not rest content even with such noble gifts as John M. Kennedy's offering of a United Charities Building at a cost of $600,000, as a headquarters for organized charity, but all shall rather see in it a proclamation of hope for every sufferer, and of summons to every child of God to give personal service in adequate measure, till the sunlight of heaven shall dispel miasma from every home of woe.

So that before long personal service, easily equal to the task in every other American city, shall not fail in Chicago, nor even in New York, whose congested population gathers into crowded limits the various forms of degraded life from many foreign lands, and across the ocean shall find some remedy for that dead sea of Liverpool, and rise to the supreme task for Charity which earth now offers in the countless multitude of London.

Love is the motive which builds into beauty and power Toynbee Hall and Oxford House, Neighborhood Guilds, Andover House and Dennison, and not surpassed by any, Hull House here at Chicago; all these college settlements, the latest and loveliest manifestation of the fierce grip which suffering and sin fasten on the sympathies of noble culture.

Love is the force which impels Brooklyn to build its Bedford Industrial Buildings and to fill them with a spirit of wisdom and sympathy which alone can save the Army of Inefficient from their impending slavery.

Love is the force which summons all whose lot is sunny to join workingmen in their strenuous demand for justice.

Love is the force to ennoble the career of the policeman into dignity, prompting him to save by friendly counsel the wild lads

---

* First used by Robert Treat Paine in his address to the Baptist Union on Dec. 29, 1879.

before their wildness issues in such crime that he must strike it down.

Love is the motive and personal service is the method by which tens of thousands of Christian Churches are to go out in their ministry not only by their thousands of priests ordained by the hand of man, but more effectively by their hundreds of thousands of men and women consecrated by the spirit of God, into every haunt of wretched life.

Repression guided by love, love re-inforced by repression, must unite to deal with every one of the various phases of the pauper problem.

Wisdom too must stand at the helm as pilot. No cause for fear when among the leaders of the social reform are the wise and strong men who are at the head of the great universities of learning. Presidents Daniel C. Gilman, of Johns Hopkins, Seth Low, of Columbia, William J. Tucker, of Dartmouth, Charles W. Elliot, of Harvard, John H. Finley, of Knox, and your own Frederick Harper at Chicago and Francis A. Walker of the Boston Institute of Technology bring to any cause they support strength and wisdom. Sociology takes rank in the colleges as a worthy study for men who propose to rule or aid their fellowmen. The rise of this study has been so rapid that only a few years ago it was introduced at Harvard as a half course, and a bit later the printer's devil would have had Prof. Peabody say that it was raised from a half curse to a whole curse. Now no college is equipped without a competent Professor of Sociology.*

Public sentiment in the community must also be aroused to take interest in all judicious movements, for instance, to support Overseers of the Poor in enforcing strict rules against lax relief, police in preventing children from begging, Boards of Health in preventing "any portion of the people from living in houses which are unfit for human habitation."

We rejoice to count as sure allies, literature and the power of the Press. If "Uncle Tom" abolished slavery, so has the "Bitter Cry" been heard round the world; "Prisoners of Poverty" must go free, "All Sorts and Conditions of Men" have their

---

* It was my hope to promote this study at Harvard as well as to strengthen this movement by the aid of thoroughly trained experts, by founding a Fellowship for Sociology.

Palace of Industry. The author's pen dipped in the blood of those who suffer, writes with power.

Nothing is more wonderful than the speed of modern events, the rapidity with which an avalanche of reform overwhelms all opposition after it has begun to move.

This International Congress of Charities meets today for the first time on the soil of America. It is honored by the counsel of illustrious men and women distinguished for philanthropic devotion from many lands.

What result, laden with larger measure of blessing for the humbler ranks of men, can issue from this Congress than a deep conviction upon all minds that the great preventible causes of human degradation can be and must be abolished?

www.ingramcontent.com/pod-product-compliance
Lightning Source LLC
Chambersburg PA
CBHW022207020726
47496CB00008B/2911